ISBN 0-86163-562-0

Text copyright Darrell Waters Limited
Illustrations copyright © 1992 Award Publications Limited

This edition first published 1992 by
Award Publications Limited, Spring House,
Spring Place, Kentish Town,
London NW5 3BH

Printed in Singapore

Enid Blyton

The Train that Lost its Way

illustrated by Dorothy Hamilton

AWARD PUBLICATIONS LIMITED

The nursery was dull and quiet. The children had gone to the seaside, and there was nobody to play with the toys.

'There's nothing to do!' said the toy clown.

'I'm bored,' said the teddy bear. 'I don't even want to growl any more.'

'Good,' said the big doll. 'I don't like your growl.'

The bear at once growled loudly.

'Mean thing,' said the big doll, and they began to quarrel.

'Something is the matter with us,' said the toy monkey. 'We are always quarrelling. Yesterday the clown pulled my tail.'

'And this morning the bear threw my key across the room,' said the clockwork mouse.

'I know what the matter is,' said the panda. 'We want a holiday! The children go away for holidays and so do the grown-ups.'

'I should like a holiday,' said the clockwork mouse. 'Let's go and get one!'

All the toys began to feel excited.

'Where shall we go?' asked the bear.

'To the seaside!' said the big doll.

'Yes let's,' said the clown.

'We'll go by train!' said the bear. 'Where's the old wooden train? Train, will you take us to the seaside in your trucks?'

'Yes, I'll take you,' said the wooden train. 'I don't know the way, but we can ask. Get in.'

'I'll be the guard,' said the clown, and he took a little green flag from the toy cupboard. He got into the last truck and beamed round at everyone.

'I'll be the driver,' said the teddy bear. 'I've always wanted to be an engine driver. Now, is everyone ready?'

The wooden train had three trucks, all of different colours.

The panda, the pink cat, the monkey and the wooden soldier got into the first truck. The big doll, the little doll and the clockwork mouse got into the second truck.

The clown was in the last truck with the blue rabbit.

'Ready?' said the clown. He waved his green flag and blew his whistle. The wooden train rumbled over the carpet to the door. They were off.

Out of the door went the train and down the passage. The garden door was open and the train rattled down a little step, almost tipping over as it went.

'Be careful!' yelled the bear. 'I almost fell out.'

Down the path went the train at top speed. It scared two sparrows into the air and made the cat jump on top of the wall in a hurry. Then it came out into the lane at the bottom of the garden. The train turned towards the south and went into a wood.

'Keep to the path, wooden train, or we'll all be jerked out!' cried the bear. On went the train down a little rabbit path and straight into a rabbit hole.

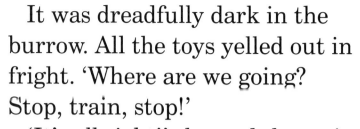

It was dreadfully dark in the burrow. All the toys yelled out in fright. 'Where are we going? Stop, train, stop!'

'It's all right!' shouted the train. 'It's only a tunnel. Don't you know that trains run through tunnels. We'll soon be out again.'

But they went deeper and deeper down, and soon they were quite lost.

The teddy bear made the train stop. 'We'll be in the middle of the earth if you go on,' he said. 'Here comes a rabbit. We'll ask him the way.'

The rabbit was very surprised to see the train in the burrow.

'You'll have to go on to Toadstool Town,' he said. 'The pixies live there. They will tell you the way to the sea.'

So on went the train again through the dark tunnel. Then, quite suddenly, out it came into the sunshine.

All round them were big toadstools. The little doll was small enough to knock at the door of one.

The pixies came crowding round the train.

'Stop here and have a meal with us,' they said. 'Then we will tell you the way to the seaside.'

So all the toys sat down and had a picnic with the pixies.

The little doll asked a pixie to give her a pair of wings.

'No. You can buy a pair in the next town, where there is a market,' she said. 'Mine wouldn't fit you.'

'Time to get on,' said the wooden train. 'All aboard, please!' And off they went, this time to the next town, to the brownie market.

As soon as the brownies saw the little doll they ran after her. 'Catch her!' they cried. 'We'll kccp hcr hcrc with us. Stay here, little doll, and you shall have a new dress and a pair of wings.'

'No, no!' cried the little doll, and she ran away fast. The wooden train rushed at the brownies, and knocked them over like skittles.

The toys piled themselves quickly into the trucks. The clown waved his flag and blew his whistle, and the train rattled off at top speed.

'I didn't buy any wings, after all,' wept the little doll. 'Oh dear, I was so frightened.'

'Sit on my knee,' said the big doll. 'You will be all right when we get to the seaside.'

But the train was in such a hurry to leave the brownies that it took the wrong road and was lost again.

It came to an enormous hill. 'You can't climb this, train!' said the teddy bear. But there was no other way to go.

Up the hill puffed the little wooden train, dragging the trucks behind it. But as soon as it reached the top of the hill, it began to rush down the other side and couldn't stop.

'There's a big pond at the bottom of the hill,' groaned the bear. 'We shall run straight into it, and sink to the bottom!'

'I want to get out!' wailed the clockwork mouse. 'I don't like going so fast.'

But SPLASH! Into the water they went. Everybody expected them to sink to the bottom and get soaking wet.

But the engine and trucks were made of wood, so of course they floated beautifully. The trucks sailed along like little boats!

There were some big white ducks on the pond. They didn't like the train splashing into their water. They sailed up, quacking angrily.

'Let's make big waves and upset them,' said one duck. But the waves took the engine and the trucks to the shore. And soon the train was on dry land again.

'Thank goodness,' said the big doll. 'Now, train, do try to go more slowly.'

The train was wet and cold and
rather tired. So it did go slowly.
It went on and on and at last ran
over some soft yellow sand.

The wheels sank into the sand,
and the train felt too tired to
drag them out. So there it stood,
quite still.

The toys got out. 'I wonder
where we are?' said the clown to
the rabbit. 'What's that noise?'

The toys could hear the sound of waves breaking, but they didn't know what it was. They all wandered about, picking up shells and bits of seaweed.

'This seems a very lonely kind of place,' said the monkey. 'And look, what is that far away down the sand? Is it water?'

'Yes. Another pond, I expect,' said the pink cat. 'Well I feel tired. I'm going to rest against a truck. You'd better come too.'

So all the toys lay down against the trucks, and fell asleep. Soon the tide came in and the waves came nearer and nearer! One wave made such a noise that it woke the monkey.

'Look!' he said. 'That pond is coming nearer. It's got waves at the edge. It's trying to reach us!'

Splash! A big wave broke and ran right to the big doll's feet. It wet her toes and she screamed.

'Quick! Let's run away!' she cried. 'The waves are going to swallow us up.'

They all pulled at the train to make it run over the sand.

'Now get in everybody!' cried the bear.

Splash! A wave ran right up to them and the train rushed away in fright. It tore up the beach and on to the road. It rattled along with all the toys holding tight.

After a long time they came to a little town. The train rushed down the street, and in at an open gateway.

'I really must have a rest,' it said. 'Get out toys, please.'

The big doll gave a cry. 'Look - we're in our own garden! There's the children's swing! Train, you brought us all the way back. However did you know?'

'My goodness,' said the bear. 'I'm glad to be home again. No more holidays for me.'

'I should have liked to see the seaside,' said the clockwork mouse.

'Never mind,' said the big doll. 'We'll go another day.'

'Yes,' said all the toys. 'And next time we shall find the way.'